A Home for
Spooky

Gloria Rand

illustrated by
Ted Rand

Henry Holt and Company • New York

Annie was riding her bike home from school when she saw a dog at the dump. It was a very skinny dog, and it was digging in the garbage.

"Hey, doggie!" she called through the fence. "What are you doing?"

The dog backed away and disappeared into the woods. Annie hurried home. She couldn't wait to tell her brother what she'd found.

LANDFILL
WARNING
CHILDREN
MUST
REMAIN in CAR

"I bet you can't guess what I found today," Annie said to Brian. "I found a dog that disappeared when I talked to it."

"Oh, right. A ghost dog." Brian rolled his eyes.

"It wasn't a ghost. It was a real dog. I wonder whose dog it is." Annie frowned. "I sure wish it were mine."

"Forget it, Annie. You know that Mom and Dad say a cat, two gerbils, and a parrot are enough pets."

"Not for me," Annie answered. "And don't you tell anyone I've found a dog. He's my secret."

"Whatever," Brian said.

The next day Annie rode past the dump again. She was hoping to see the dog, and there it was, peeking out at her from behind thick weeds that grew alongside the road.

"I bet you can't guess what I found today," Annie said to Brian. "I found a dog that disappeared when I talked to it."

"Oh, right. A ghost dog." Brian rolled his eyes.

"It wasn't a ghost. It was a real dog. I wonder whose dog it is." Annie frowned. "I sure wish it were mine."

"Forget it, Annie. You know that Mom and Dad say a cat, two gerbils, and a parrot are enough pets."

"Not for me," Annie answered. "And don't you tell anyone I've found a dog. He's my secret."

"Whatever," Brian said.

The next day Annie rode past the dump again. She was hoping to see the dog, and there it was, peeking out at her from behind thick weeds that grew alongside the road.

Annie put her bike down and tiptoed toward the dog.

"Hey, Spooky. You don't mind if I call you Spooky, do you? You really need a name."

Annie held out a piece of cookie. "Here, boy, don't be scared of me. I just want to give you a little treat." Spooky wagged his tail, but he didn't come out of his hiding place.

Annie rode by the dump every day. Every day Spooky was there, and every day Annie called to him. At first, Spooky stayed in the weeds and watched her. Finally, one day he poked his head out.

Soon after that Spooky came to Annie when she called. He would eat a cookie, half a sandwich, or a piece of fruit right out of her hand. He even let Annie pat his head.

"You are so skinny," Annie said as she rubbed Spooky's back. "You're scared of everything, and you're almost too weak to walk. You need me to take care of you, don't you?"

Annie spent a lot of time with Spooky. She brought him food she'd saved from her lunch. And she carried water for him in a plastic bottle and poured it into an old bowl she'd brought from home.

"What's going on?" Annie's mother asked her one afternoon. "You're coming home from school later and later every day. On weekends you're hardly here at all."

Annie just shrugged.

"Nothing, Mom," she said.

A few days later Annie found Spooky lying next to the road. "Spooky, what are you doing?" she asked. "Is something the matter with you? Come on, stand up."

Spooky didn't move. Annie climbed onto her bike and pedaled home as fast as she could.

"Mom! Dad! Spooky is sick! He's really sick!" Annie called as she ran into the house.

"Spooky?" her mother said. "What are you talking about?"

"Oh, it's Annie's ghost dog," Brian said with a smirk. "Spooky is Annie's big secret."

"He isn't a ghost," Annie said, sobbing. "And you weren't supposed to tell."

Annie told her parents about Spooky and how he depended on her.

"Everyone get into the car," her father said after Annie had finished her story. "It's nearly dark and we need to find that dog right away."

Spooky was not where Annie had left him, so with flashlights in hand, Annie and her family began to search for him. They found paths Spooky had made through the woods, little dugouts where he had rested, and pieces of paper that had held scraps of food he'd brought out from the dump. But they didn't find Spooky until Annie heard him whimpering.

"Hey, Spooky, don't be scared. It's just me and my family," Annie said as she gently pulled Spooky out from under a bush. "We've come to take you home."

"It's a good thing you told us about Spooky when you did, Annie," her father said as he carefully carried Spooky to the car. "You were right. He's very sick. We've got to get him to a doctor."

Annie held Spooky's head on her lap as they drove to the animal hospital.

"Well, what have we here?" the doctor asked as he lifted Spooky onto an examining table.

"His name is Spooky," Annie said. "I found him at the dump."

The doctor looked serious. "My goodness," he said. "This dog hasn't had the right kind of food for a long time. He's suffering from starvation. A lost or abandoned pet like Spooky usually can't survive long on its own."

Under the bright hospital lights, Spooky looked worse than ever to Annie. His eyes were sunken, his ribs stuck out, and he could barely move.

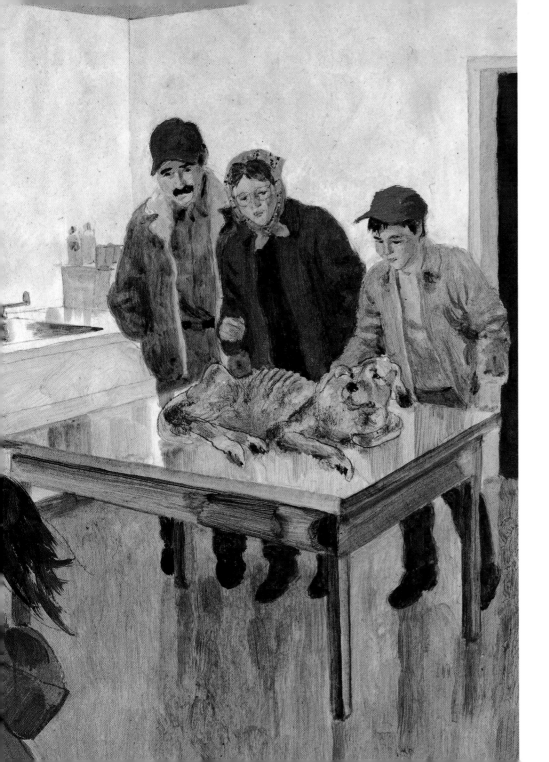

"The kindest thing to do for this dog," the doctor said, "would be for me to give him a shot that would help him die painlessly."

"No. Don't do that," Annie pleaded. " I know Spooky can get well."

"I want Spooky to live, too," the doctor said, "but even with good care, it's doubtful he'll recover. I'll give him the right medicine and the right food and we'll see how he is in a couple of days."

Annie leaned over and patted Spooky. "You have to get well," she whispered to him. Spooky looked at Annie with sad but trusting eyes.

Spooky was a good patient. He took the medicine and ate the food the doctor gave him, and he drank lots of water.

Annie visited Spooky every day.

Slowly Spooky began to get better. One day he surprised Annie. He was strong enough to wag his tail again. A few days later he was strong enough to take a walk.

The doctor smiled at Annie. "I have good news," he said. "After Spooky gets a bath and a final checkup tomorrow, he can go home."

The next day Annie arrived at the hospital with a present for Spooky. It was a new red collar with a special tag. On the tag were Spooky's name and his new address.

When the doctor brought Spooky into the waiting room, Spooky ran to Annie, yelping excitedly.

Annie gave Spooky a big hug. "Are you ready to come live at my house?" she asked him.

Spooky jumped up, put his paws on Annie's shoulders, and licked her face.

Then, together they hurried out the door and headed for home.

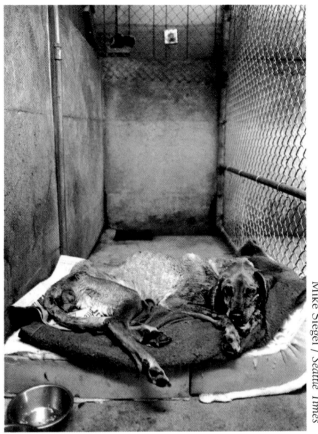

Mike Siegel / Seattle Times

Mike Siegel / Seattle Times

Author's Note

The story of Spooky is based on the rescue of a real dog. This starving part hound, part mutt was found wandering near a landfill dump by Linda Buskirk, a veterinarian's assistant. For months she and her family tried to coax the dog they'd named Hope to come home with them, but Hope was scared and hid whenever they came too close to her.

Even with food and water left every day by the Buskirks, Hope continued to grow thinner and sicker. Finally, with the help of a determined animal-control officer, Hope was captured and brought to the clinic where Linda worked.

Ted Rand

    The story of Hope's will to live was featured on television and in local newspapers. Get-well cards came from schoolchildren, and money donated for her care was banked in an account called the Hope Chest.

    For weeks Hope barely hung on to life, but with tender, loving care and the best of veterinary medicine, she slowly gained strength. After a long and often uncomfortable recovery, a happy and healthy Hope was adopted by the Buskirks and moved into a beautiful new doghouse they built just for her.

To Marge and Ray Perry for their love of animals and
support of the Humane Society.   —G.R. and T.R.

Henry Holt and Company, Inc.
Publishers since 1866
115 West 18th Street
New York, New York 10011

Henry Holt is a registered trademark of Henry Holt and Company, Inc.

Published in Canada by Fitzhenry & Whiteside Ltd.,
195 Allstate Parkway, Markham, Ontario L3R 4T8.

Library of Congress Cataloging-in-Publication Data
Rand, Gloria.
A home for Spooky / Gloria Rand; illustrations by Ted Rand.
Summary: Based on a true story, a girl finds a homeless dog in
a dump, visits him every day, and eventually saves his life.
 [1. Dogs—Fiction.] I. Rand, Ted, ill. II. Title.
PZ7.R1553Ho 1997 [E]—dc21 97-18573

ISBN 0-8050-4611-9
First Edition—1998
Typography by Meredith Baldwin

The artist used grease pencil and acrylics on 100 percent rag paper
to create the illustrations for this book.
Printed in the United States of America on acid-free paper. ∞
10 9 8 7 6 5 4 3 2 1

E
R

Rand, Gloria.

A home for Spooky.

$15.95

DATE			
5/4 KL			
6/4 12G			
4/10 1B			